# *Dear Parent:*
# *Your child's love of reading starts here!*

Every child learns to read in a different way and at his or her own speed. Some go back and forth between reading levels and read favorite books again and again. Others read through each level in order. You can help your young reader improve and become more confident by encouraging his or her own interests and abilities. From books your child reads with you to the first books he or she reads alone, there are I Can Read Books for every stage of reading:

## SHARED READING
Basic language, word repetition, and whimsical illustrations, ideal for sharing with your emergent reader

## BEGINNING READING
Short sentences, familiar words, and simple concepts for children eager to read on their own

## READING WITH HELP
Engaging stories, longer sentences, and language play for developing readers

## READING ALONE
Complex plots, challenging vocabulary, and high-interest topics for the independent reader

## ADVANCED READING
Short paragraphs, chapters, and exciting themes for the perfect bridge to chapter books

**I Can Read Books** have introduced children to the joy of reading since 1957. Featuring award-winning authors and illustrators and a fabulous cast of beloved characters, I Can Read Books set the standard for beginning readers.

A lifetime of discovery begins with the magical words **"I Can Read!"**

Visit www.icanread.com for information on enriching your child's reading experience

**Fayetteville Free Library**
**300 Orchard Street**
**Fayetteville, NY 13066**

I Can Read Book® is a trademark of HarperCollins Publishers.

The Voyage of the *Dawn Treader:* Quest for the Lost Lords Text copyright © 2010 by C.S. Lewis Pte. Ltd. Photographs copyright ©
2010 by Twentieth Century Fox Film Corporation and Walden Media, LLC. All rights reserved. Printed in the United States of America.
No part of this book may be used or reproduced in any manner whatsoever without written permission except in the case of brief quota-
tions embodied in critical articles and reviews. For information address HarperCollins Children's Books, a division of HarperCollins
Publishers, 10 East 53rd Street, New York, NY 10022.
www.icanread.com

Library of Congress catalog card number: 2010929547
ISBN 978-0-06-196908-9

Typography by Rick Farley

10 11 12 13 14 LP/WOR 10 9 8 7 6 5 4 3 2 1

❖

First Edition

# I Can Read!

READING 2 WITH HELP

## THE CHRONICLES OF NARNIA
### THE VOYAGE OF THE DAWN TREADER

## Quest for the Lost Lords

Adapted by Jennifer Frantz

Based on the screenplay by
Christopher Markus & Steve McFeely
and Michael Petroni

Based on the book by C. S. Lewis

**HARPER**

*An Imprint of HarperCollinsPublishers*

"Keep swimming!"
Edmund shouted
to his sister Lucy
and his cousin Eustace.

They were in the middle
of the ocean near a huge ship.

Moments before,
the three cousins were looking
at a painting of a ship
in Eustace's house.

"The water's moving," Lucy had said.

"It is not. Stop it!" Eustace whined.

But Lucy was right!

Suddenly water was everywhere.

The children were pulled

through the painting

into the ocean.

Edmund and Lucy had seen this kind

of magic before—in Narnia!

"Hang on!" a man

on the ship shouted.

The children were fished out
of the ocean by the ship's crew.

The ship was the *Dawn Treader*.

It belonged to Lucy and Edmund's
friend Caspian, King of Narnia.

"Edmund! Lucy!" Caspian shouted.

He was surprised and happy

to see his two friends.

He told them he was sailing

to the Lone Islands to find

the seven lost lords of Narnia.

The *Dawn Treader*'s first stop
was Narrowhaven.

Caspian, Lucy, Edmund
and the others went ashore
to investigate.

But evil men were waiting for them!

Narrowhaven was full of

wicked slave traders.

The children were captured.

Lucy and Eustace were taken away

to be sold as slaves.

Caspian and Edmund were
thrown into a dungeon.

At the slave market,

Lucy and Eustace

were about to be sold.

"I'll take them," a voice said.

It was one of Caspian's

loyal Narnians!

Lucy and Eustace were saved.

The dungeon guards

were distracted

by the noise below.

"Now!" Edmund said to Caspian.

They rushed the guards and broke free.

During their escape,
the children found someone
very important.

"Lord Bern!" Caspian said.

The man was one of

the seven lost lords of Narnia!

Lord Bern showed Caspian
his old sword.
"A gift from Aslan
to protect Narnia," he said.

Caspian, Edmund and Lucy

vowed to find the other lost lords.

They would stop at nothing.

This was the reason Narnia

had called Lucy and Edmund back.

As they sailed off,

Lucy and Edmund were happy

to be back with their friend Caspian

in the place they loved most.

"For Narnia!" they shouted.